THE TEDDY BEARS' PICNIC

By Jimmy Kennedy
Illustrated by Alexandra Day

ALADDIN PAPERBACKS
New York London Toronto Sydney Singapore

The artist wishes to thank
Rabindranath Darling and Elizabeth Ratisseau
for permitting their bears
to pose for these paintings.

First Aladdin Paperbacks edition June 2000

Words copyright © 1907 by M. Witmark & Sons
Used by permission of Warner Bros. Music
Illustrations copyright © 1983 by Alexandra Day

Aladdin Paperbacks
An imprint of Simon & Schuster Children's Publishing Division
1230 Avenue of the Americas
New York, NY 10020

The Library of Congress has cataloged the hardcover edition as follows:
Kennedy, Jim.
The teddy bears' picnic / by Jim Kennedy ; illustrated by Alexandra Day.
p.   cm.
Summary: This decades-old song describes the teddy bears' grand picnic in the woods.
ISBN 978-0-671-75589-8 (hc.)
1. Children's songs—Texts. 2. Teddy bears—Songs and music. 3. Picnicking—Songs and music. 4. Songs.
I. Day, Alexandra, ill. II. Title.
PZ8.3.K383 Te 1991
[E] dc—20
91-24944   CIP AC
ISBN 978-0-689-83530-8 (Aladdin pbk.)
0117 SCP

If you go down in the woods today
You're sure of a big surprise

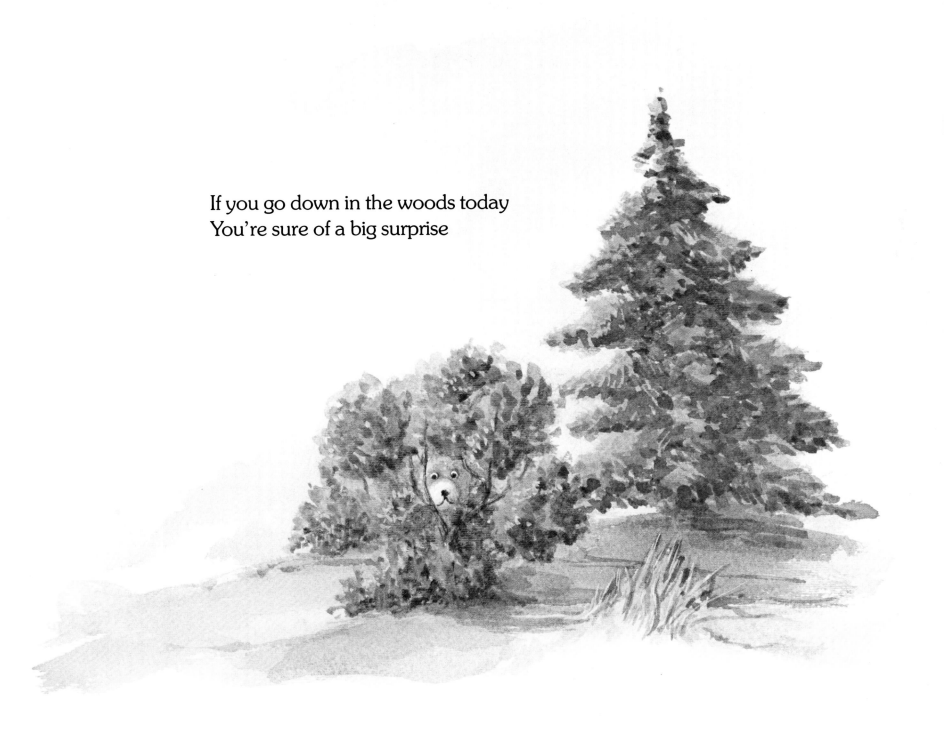

If you go down in the woods today
You'd better go in disguise

For every bear that ever there was

Will gather there for certain because

Today's the day the Teddy Bears have their picnic.

Every Teddy Bear who's been good
Is sure of a treat today
There's lots of marvelous things to eat
And wonderful games to play

Beneath the trees where nobody sees
They'll hide and seek as long as they please
'Cause that's the way the Teddy Bears have their picnic.

If you go down
    in the woods today

You'd better not go alone

It's lovely down
    in the woods today

But safer to stay at home

For every Bear that ever there was
Will gather there for certain because
Today's the day the Teddy Bears have their picnic.

Picnic time for Teddy Bears
The little Teddy Bears are having a lovely time today

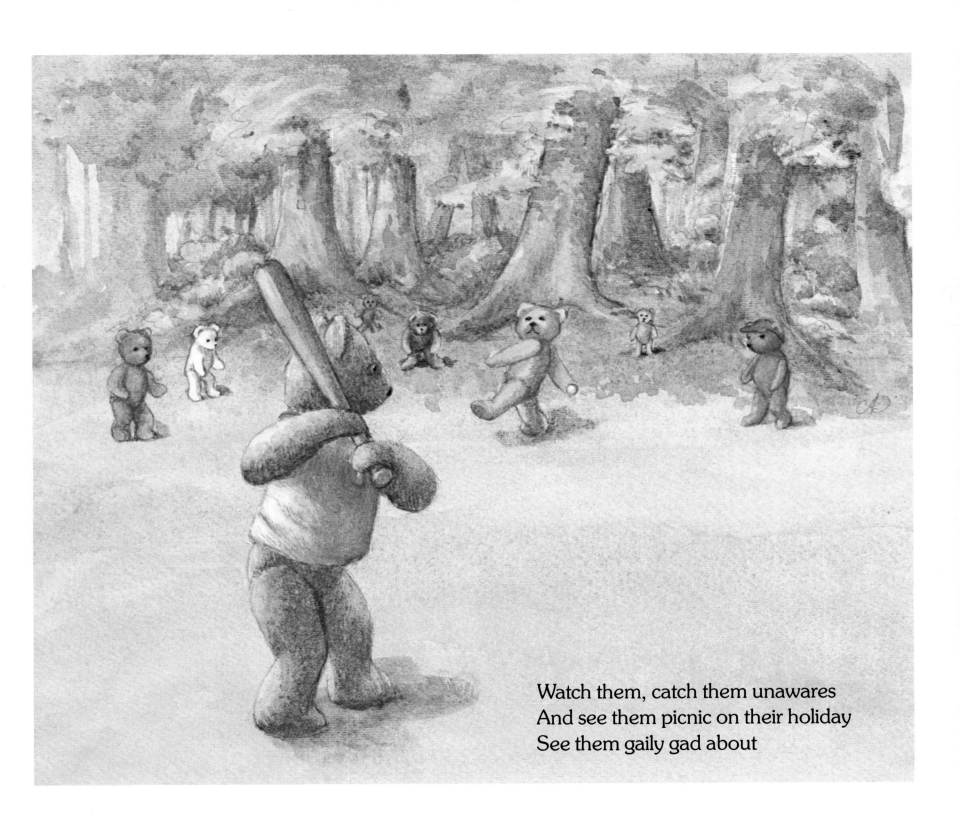

Watch them, catch them unawares
And see them picnic on their holiday
See them gaily gad about

They love to play and shout

They never have any care

At six o'clock their mummys and daddys
Will take them home to bed

Because they're tired little Teddy Bears.

The paintings for this book were executed in egg tempera.
The type is Souvenir Light set by Eucalyptus Productions, Inc. of San Diego.
Color separations by Photolitho AG, Gossau-Zurich, Switzerland.
Manufactured in China.